P9-CRQ-166

This book was purchased from
GoodMinds.com
First Nations, Métis, Inuit Books
Bound to Impress
To Re-Order 1.877.862.8483/www.goodminds.com

POWWOW'S COMING

LINDA BOYDEN

University of New Mexico Press
ALBUQUERQUE

For my father, Raymond E. Simmons Sr.,
and my Simmons family,
Lee and Loretta Burkitt, and the Maui Chapter
of the Intertribal Council of Hawaii,
and Noah, for believing first.

Special thanks to UNM Press, Debbi Smith,
Janet Bassett, my children and grandchildren,
and as always, to my husband, John.

Published 2007
Printed and bound in Malaysia through TWP America, Inc.

17 16 15 14 13 4 5 6 7 8

Library of Congress Cataloging-in-Publication Data

Boyden, Linda.
Powwow's coming / Linda Boyden.
p. cm.
ISBN 978-0-8263-4265-2 (cloth : alk. paper)
1. Powwows—Juvenile literature. I. Title.

E98.P86B68 2007
394'.3—dc22

2007008923

Book composition by Damien Shay
Body type is ITC Lubalin Graph 20/30 ~ Display type is Bureau Eagle

WHY WE DANCE

To dance is to pray
to pray is to heal
to heal is to give
to give is to live
to live is to dance.

—MariJo Moore © 2004

Powwow's coming,
hear the beat?

Powwow's coming,
dancing feet.

Powwow's coming,
hear the drum?

Powwow's coming . . .

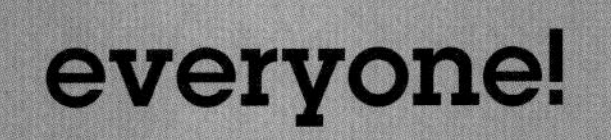
everyone!

Build the booths
and
vendors' stalls.

Sort the wares
and
stack them tall.

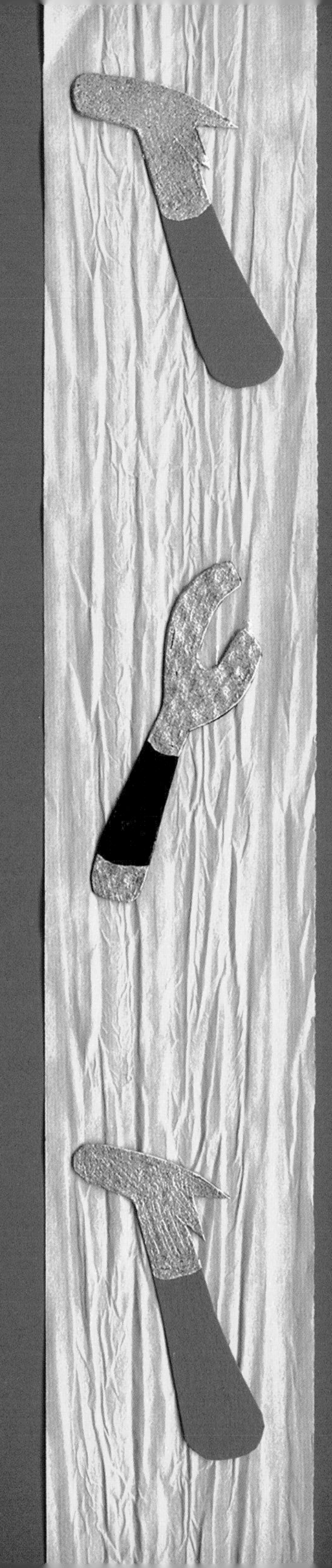

Aunty Dot's
MAUI
POW WOW

**Many hands,
the work goes fast.**

**Powwow time
is here at last!**

Powwow's coming, hear the beat?
Powwow's coming, dancing feet.
Powwow's coming, hear the drum?
Powwow's coming, everyone!
BOYDEN
Powwow's Coming
Powwow's Coming
LINDA BOYDEN

"Powwows started
long ago,
but dances change,
powwows grow.

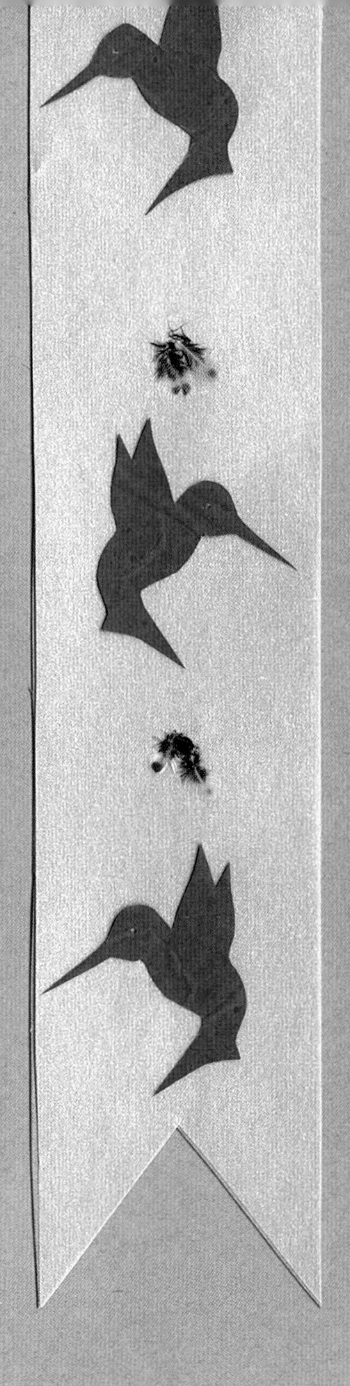

“Still today the
steps and songs
bless the dancers,
make them strong.

"At powwows
far away from here,
people travel
every year.

Hundreds watch
the dancers try
to do their best,
to win a prize.

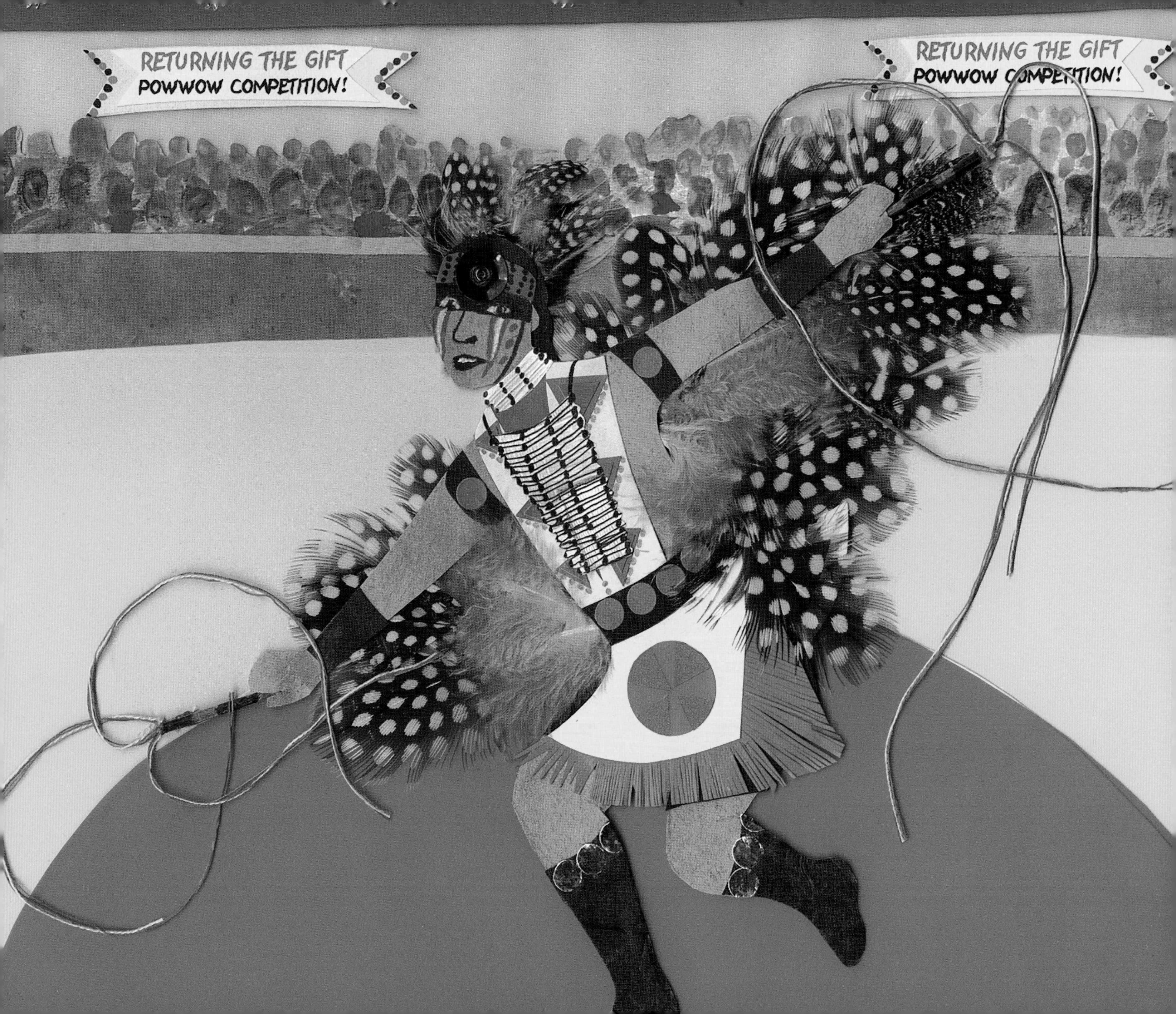
RETURNING THE GIFT
POWWOW COMPETITION!
RETURNING THE GIFT
POWWOW COMPETITION!

Often, powwows
can be small,
we work together,
one and all.

For graduations,
birthdays, too,
or when family visits,
just like you!”

WELCOME HOME!
N.D.N
TACOS
FRYBREAD

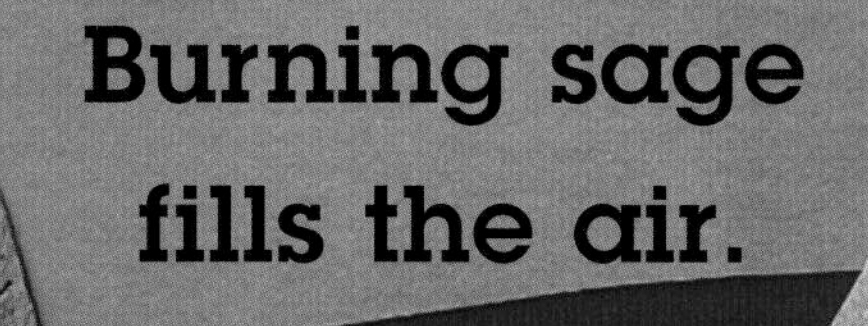

Burning sage
fills the air.

Dancers, workers
smudge with care.

Braids are tightened, laces tied.
Elders nod with smiles and pride.

Fringe on shawls
sways and swings.

Jingle dresses
chime and ring.

Grass dancers
step and prance
to the rhythms
of the dance.

Shoppers look
in vendors' stalls:

Flutes and feathers,
masks and dolls,
frybread, tacos,
venison stew.

Lots to see,
lots to do.

LEE & LORETTA'S
FRY BREAD! 2 SCRIPS
N*D*N TACO-3 SCRIPS
ICE CREAM-2 SCRIPS
WATER or SODA-1 SCRIP
CODE TALKER

Storytellers spin and weave
tales of fun and mystery.

In the Game Booth,
try to win
at Hubbub's Toss
or Ring and Pin.

The sun slips low,
to the west;
dancers, workers
did their best.

Giveaways in
grateful hands,
friendships made
from many lands.

Powwow's ending,
slow the beat.

Powwow's ending,
tired feet.

Powwow's ending,
silent drum.

Powwow smiles
on everyone!

NOTE TO THE READER

WHAT IS A POWWOW? A powwow is a Native American gathering held for many reasons. Some powwows celebrate an event like a graduation or a birthday. Others honor veterans, elders, or Native traditions such as a naming ceremony or an annual harvest. Many large powwows are times for dance competitions. No matter what its reason, a powwow is always a time for American Indian people to come together and remember their tribal traditions, to discuss the future, to spend time with family and friends, and to let the heartbeat of the drum renew their spirits.

HOW TO BEHAVE AT A POWWOW?
Etiquette varies from event to event. Be mindful of the unique differences between different cultures, but the following are general guidelines:

- Listen to the Master of Ceremonies and honor all his requests, particularly to stand (if physically able to), or to maintain silence during certain times to show respect.
- Never walk across the arena circle.
- Ask individual dancers and drum groups for permission to photograph or record them in any way, including cell phone cameras.
- Please do not touch a dancer's regalia without permission.
- Most powwows do not allow smoking, drugs, or alcohol.
- Respect elders.
- When in doubt about the right thing to do, ask a powwow volunteer/committee member who would be happy to help.
- Enjoy!

GAMES! Games are an important part of Native American traditions, and hopefully a fun part of your family traditions, too. Games teach you how to take turns and play fair, how to win without bragging, and how to lose without tears. Two games are mentioned in this book, although there are many more American Indian games. To learn more, check out *Native American Games and Stories* by James Bruchac and Joseph Bruchac from Fulcrum Publishing: www.fulcrum-resources.com.

Hubbub

Many tribes have had variations of Hubbub, a lively game of chance. It can be played with two people or two teams (much more fun!).

MATERIALS:
- A blanket for the players to sit on.
- A shallow bowl or basket, twelve inches round.
- Five round "dice" made of wood, bone, dried peach pits, or my favorite, small flat stones. The dice need to be painted black on one side and unmarked on the other so to be of two colors (it's okay to paint the dice a different color on each side).
- Fifty-three counters; fifty-two are nine-inch sticks (craft sticks, twigs, or pieces of cardboard) and the last one is slightly larger and shaped like an arrow, called the Sagamon.

INSTRUCTIONS:
Choose one person to be the Lodgekeeper, who then is the referee and in charge of the sticks. Other players sit in a circle on the blanket and take turns holding the basket with the stones. The Player holds the basket tightly and shakes it gently while the rest of the players call, "Hub, hub, hub, hub, HUB!" (the last hub should be shouted). When HUB is shouted, the Player must snap the basket onto the blanket, forcing the stones up in the air. All of the dice must land BACK IN THE BASKET or there is no score and the Player loses his turn. If the Player catches the dice, the Lodgekeeper looks at the dice in the basket and determines the score and gives out sticks.

SCORING:
- 4 of one color, 1 of the other = no score, no sticks.
- 3 of one color, 2 of the other = 2 sticks.
- 5 of one color = 4 sticks or, if the sticks are all gone, the Player receives the Sagamon stick, thus winning the game.

If the Player earns sticks, she can keep having a turn until making no score. Game is ended when the sticks are all given out and a player wins the Sagamon stick, which can only be won with ALL 5 dice on the same color IN ONE TOSS, which is harder to do than you think.

Ring and Pin

MATERIALS:
A straight stick (a twig or wooden chopsticks broken in half) about twelve inches long, string or yarn (approximately eighteen inches or longer), and a pipe cleaner. Form the pipe cleaner into a small circle. Tie one end of the yarn/string to the circle, then tie the other end onto the stick.

RULES:
- First decide how many points will make the game (I like to start with ten and then work up to higher numbers).
- Players take turns, one is the Watcher and one is the Flipper.
- The Flipper can only use one hand to hold the stick. Put your other hand behind your back.
- The Flipper swings the string and flips it up, trying to catch the hoop on the stick.
- Your turn is over if you don't catch your hoop. You earn one point if you do catch the hoop.
- Game continues until the first player earns the agreed upon points.